COLLECTED

PRIDEAUX

GHOST STORIES

A CIP catalogue record for this title is

available from the British Library.

ISBN 978-0-9954609-4-2

www.paganuspublishing.co.uk

First Published in 2017

Paganus Publishing

Ruthin

Denbighshire

Paganus Publishing 2017

STORY DESCRIPTION

Collected Prideaux Ghost Stories is another in the series of Prideaux ghost stories. It follows the book **More Prideaux Ghost Stories** and precedes **A Christmas Story.**

Each story features a generation of the family in my line. The people, houses, villages and timelines are correct in each story. Some features of the stories have either been passed down or added by the author with a great deal of poetic licence.

The Starling Tree features John Prideaux. He runs from his birth town of Chudleigh after experiencing the terrible fire which occurred there. His travels take him to Leeds and London and he learns that bad thoughts and deeds do create things which may have affected his life in ways he could not have foretold.

Christmas at the Workhouse features Matthew Prideaux. A life of poverty and death did not stop him educating himself through his own efforts. During his final hours on Christmas Night 1887 he has a conversation with a young school teacher. As she takes notes about conditions in the workhouse she soon learns that not everyone who dies has left the building.

Cherry Ripe features George Herbert Prideaux. A chance meeting with the prison guards who had attended a hanging at Armley Gaol sends George on a path which altered his whole life.

CAST LIST

As with the other Prideaux Ghost Stories books, names are repeated regularly and I find it helpful to differentiate between the Prideauxs in order to lessen irritation and the constant cry from the reader of, 'which Prideaux is she talking about now?'
Remember that these characters not only existed but are ancestors of mine.

The Starling Tree – John Prideaux (1796-1863)

Married Elizabeth Lock on 18th October 1824 – died 24th June 1837
Charity born 28th February 1825 – died 24th June 1837
Edwin John born 4th October 1833
Married Mary 1837 – died 1864
Matthew born 1838

Christmas at the Workhouse – Matthew Prideaux (1838 – 1888)

Married Sarah Jackson 1863 – died 1884
Mary Emma born 1865
Agnes Jane born 1867
Edwin John born 1868
George Herbert born 1871
William born 1873
Albert born 1875 – died 1876
Thomas Alfred born 1878

Twin Eliza born 4th September 1880 – died 1882
Twin Charles Edward born 4th September 1880 – died 17th September 1880

Cherry Ripe – George Herbert Prideaux (1871 – 1926)

Married Mary Ann Hobson on 21st January 1893
George born 1893
Arthur born 1894
Annie born 1895
Benjamin 1898 – died Christmas Eve 1899
Jane born 1900
Clifford born Christmas Day 1902
Herbert born 1907
Wilfred born 1912

CONTENTS

STORY DESCRIPTION 6

CAST LIST 8

CONTENTS...10

THE STARLING TREE..12

    featuring John Prideaux 1796- 1863 12

CHRISTMAS AT THE WORKHOUSE 37

    featuring Matthew Prideaux 1838 -1888 37

CHERRY RIPE 62

    featuring George Prideaux 1871 – 1926...................62

THE STARLING TREE

featuring John Prideaux 1796- 1863

John was surprised that he was remembering so far back, even though the pain and visual sights were so current and so painful. He could see the broken railing through which he had just fallen and the heavy rain now splashing onto his cold and paralysed body, but he was remembering the difficult path he had travelled which had resulted in this sad event.

The 22nd May 1807 was an exciting day for John Prideaux even though it probably wasn't for neither his family nor indeed his hometown of Chudleigh.
It was a Friday.
He was sitting in school staring at the teacher, Mr Bond. John usually enjoyed school but today was so hot that his usually quick mind was stuck in stall mode. He winked at his friend Elizabeth Lock, and she grinned back.
Suddenly the door was thrown open and a frightened looking child stood wide eyed in the space it left.
"What is the meaning of this intrusion?" shouted Mr Bond.
"A fire sir. There is a fire!" said the little boy.
"Where?" asked the teacher.

"Everywhere sir. The town is on fire. I think my house is on fire," and the boy began to cry.

John felt his heart beat quickly. Did that mean his house was on fire?

"Sir, sir, can I go home and see if my mother is alright?" he asked. There was a great clamour of voices asking similar questions.

"No, no, no. Sit down class; you must all remain here where it is safe."

Mr Bond was beginning to worry.

"In fact, stay here class and I shall go out and see what is happening."

Mr Bond left the room and as soon as he did, John climbed onto a table and looked out of the window. He saw black smoke and flames coming from the town and he could hear screaming. That was it, he wasn't staying a moment longer.

John ran out of the door and outside onto the street. The rest of the class watched and some followed him, while the timid stayed behind.

The sight which met his eyes was one he had never forgotten. Around him was a mixture of black and yellow and red and there was no sky. The air was choking and people were running in no particular direction. Everything seemed to be on fire.

He ran in the direction of his house past all the familiar sights which were now ablaze. No one spoke to him or tried to stop him. He thought he saw a dead horse across the street, but did not stop to find out.

When he reached the site of his house he was horrified to see his mother and father standing in front of their cottage with baby Peter and some of their belongings in the cart.

"Mother?" he said.

"Oh John," she pulled him towards her body and hugged him while she cried.

"Is everyone all right?" he asked, his voice shaking.

"I think so. Did you leave your brothers and sister at school?"

John said nothing, he had not checked before he left. He had been too concerned about his mother.

"Yes," he answered.

As soon as his mother let him go, John saw that they were never going to rescue his home. It was in the path of the fire which was now two houses away, it was all going to go. As the first flames hit, he saw the black, many legged creatures running along the beams and away from the heat. At first he thought they were rats but they were more like giant spiders, so he ran away because they reminded him of the sleepless nights he had spent listening to clog scurrying.

Elizabeth caught up with him.

"I was worried about you John."

"My house has burnt to the ground and we have lost everything," he announced.

Elizabeth's face fell.

"How horrible. What about your family?"

"They are alright, I think. Have you seen the town?"

"They fetched me and told me to stay here. I saw the smoke and the flames, but they won't let me come out."

"You can't miss this Elizabeth, come out with me now. I will look after you, they will never know."

"I will come, they are all busy looking after themselves and trying to save the house, but I think we are too far away."

Mary jumped out of the window and went with her friend.

They ran across the grass and had to stop as a carriage began to turn in front of them. These coaches travelling with passengers from Plymouth to Exeter usually went through the centre of the town, but today were diverting around the back of the town through the dry fields.

"Are you alright?" shouted the driver.

"Yes thank you," they answered.

 The two giggled because drivers never spoke to them usually.

The town was even more ablaze. Men were pulling down houses in order to stop the fire. It was very exciting for the children with buildings crashing down and people crying. They watched until after four o' clock when the fire seemed to be mainly out. Lord Clifford came into the town and sent word around that anyone could come to Ugbrooke.

By evening men and women came from other villages to help and the army sent tents.

The Prideaux family were to spend the night under one of these tents and Thomas was likely to be given more work to rebuild the town, he told his wife. John remembered that his parents would argue a lot about how he came to get the work. They did move to the farm about which his mother always talked prior to the fire. Apparently there was a large insurance pay out and they got to keep the Fore Street property too which they developed later. It was a very convenient fire for his family and few others too.

John followed in his father's footsteps and learned the carpentry trade as did his brothers. He was a very handsome young man and he enjoyed much female attention. Elizabeth had moved away with her family and so he entertained himself with the local beauties. That was until a chance meeting with Elizabeth at Exeter resulted in a more mature renewal of friendship and ultimately romance.

She had sent John a note telling him that she was with child and they had decided to run away to London. After telling his parents that they were to marry, Charity had become hysterical and said that this was a trap women liked to set for men.

John and his brother Peter had heard stories of London and how a man could get rich quite easily there. Other town people had gone there in the past and as time went on the young men decided to seek their fortune. So at the end of summer in he persuaded Peter to come with them.

"Please, please don't go!" begged their mother.

"Let them go if they want. They can always come home if it doesn't work out," said Thomas.

"If they go, I will never see them again," cried Charity, unconsciously repeating the cries of Thomas's own mother when Charity had encouraged him to leave Ringmore all those years ago. She was correct, they left Chudleigh for London and they never returned. They did not write and no word ever came back. Charity was devastated.

She did not know that they went first to Landkey near Bideford where John married the pregnant Elizabeth Locke in front of his brother and her family on Monday the 18th October 1824 one week before they went to London. Edwin Locke had a property there which he wanted managing by family. It fronted as a General Store but was used as a place to launder the spoils of burglary and murder. There was a great deal of money to be made.

But when they arrived in London, it was not all that they had expected. Used as they were to Devon and considering Exeter to be extremely busy, particularly on market days, London was horribly congested. It was filthy, smelly and full of violence and crime. John and Peter lost some of their possessions as soon as they arrived, although thankfully Elizabeth was spared. Several people of questionable moral intent frequented the shop. They brought small items mainly, some valuable and some not so much. The shopkeeper, who

went home after the shop shut and was called Jedidiah
Winthrop, was a dirty and insolent man. However he
appeared to know the valuable of the property brought
in by equally scary vagabonds.

"Edwin Locke will go through all of these accounts when
he arrives but twice a year and God help us if it doesn't
all add up," Jed told John.

Peter Prideaux got fed up pretty quickly of the place
and soon found lodgings and a job with a builder.

As Elizabeth grew in size, she became more frightened
and complained that sometimes one or two of the men
would make lewd comments to her. John was
apoplectic when he heard this news and threatened to
beat the man to a pulp. It took almost an hour for Jed to
talk him out of it, warning him that John was likely to
end up dead and thrown into the stinking river.

He and Elizabeth went for a walk one night by the river
when the baby was only about a week away. They saw
drunks, tarts and children stealing from the gents who
were busy with the tarts.

"We must leave London," Elizabeth told her husband. "I
am not bringing up a child here."

"We should give it a bit longer. At least until your father
comes and then we can see how much we have earned.
He promised us a good cut and the amount of money
changing hands here is a fortune. We can set up on our
own in no time."

"But I can't breathe here John. London chokes me."

Their daughter Charity was born in London and a letter
was sent to Devon - to the Locke's. Edwin arrived a
month later and soon after he discussed money and
business with John.

"I thought I would be making more than this. There is a
lot of risk involved."

"I managed before you got here, you have a roof over
your head and that it is a bonus in this city. Be grateful
for that."

Locke shooed   him away and huddled with Jed. Locke
seemed menacing in this environment and so John went
upstairs to his wife and child and told her that they
would be in London a while yet.

They were awoken later when the front door was kicked
in and several men ran upstairs and into their room.
Elizabeth picked up Charity and held her to her bosom
while John fought them in vain. By the time they left,
John was badly beaten and Edwin was dead. Jed had
vanished and the house was on fire. It was soon made
clear that Lockes were out of business and John and his
family must leave London or face the consequences.

So leave London they did and travelled to Staley Bridge
where Elizabeth had heard that there might be some
honest work. John told the villagers that he was a
journeyman carpenter and work was soon found for
him .No one enquired after his past. The family were
happy and grew happier still when they had a son Edwin
John a few years later. Life was quite normal until John

had begun to notice the tree - not long after moving into his cottage.

To all intents and purposes it was just an ordinary tree. A good old English oak tree with squirrels and owls and acorns hanging from its branches. It was a particularly splendid tree and on the first day they moved there John saw a starling which they laughingly said seemed to be watching them.

The next day there were two sitting there. They laughed about that too and every day for a week as the starlings continued to arrive. The starlings would sit next to each other on the branches and do nothing. They sat quietly and never left the tree. John was pretty sure that they stayed overnight as he never seemed to see them leaving or arriving for that matter.

At first it was funny and they would take breadcrumbs and other small leftovers outside for their pet birds. They commented that they never saw the starlings leave the branches but whenever they looked for the crumbs, there was none to be found.

"Perhaps they sucked them up with their willpower, they look capable enough," laughed Elizabeth.

"I wonder where they are all coming from?" asked John.

"And why?" asked Elizabeth which was a better question.

By the time Edwin John was born, there were several hundred silent starlings sitting in the tree. Neighbours had begun to notice the phenomenon and after initially laughing, soon began to talk in whispers about the Devil and hauntings.

"This has never happened before," said one.

"It goes against nature," added another.

The parson arrived one morning following Edwin's birth in order to arrange the baptism.

"There are a lot of birds in your tree Mistress Elizabeth," he said softly.

"I assume that is not a euphemism Parson."

The parson was shocked and he wasn't really sure whether it was because she knew what a euphemism was or that she had said it.

"No. I merely thought it strange that so many starlings should remain in one place."

"I am not a witch if that is what you are inferring."

"Indeed I am not. I am making conversation while we arrange the baptism of your son. I presume little Charity was baptised in London?"

"She was not sir but we do want Edwin baptising."

"But you must baptise your daughter too!" more shocked than he thought he could be, the parson sat down.

"I shall if you let me know how that will be possible."

He told her and the deed was arranged for the following Sunday. He felt he must do this as quickly as possible before the Devil got hold of these Prideauxs and their children. As he left, he noticed that the silent starlings had now begun a synchronised chirrup and the tree seemed to vibrate with the sound. He pulled his cloak hood over his head and scurried away until the sound was no longer with him.

Elizabeth came out of the house and looked up at the tree. Charity clung to her hand and Edwin clutched her bosom. There were so many starlings in the tree, she could scarcely make out leaf or twig. As she looked the sound stopped and all was silent. She shivered and ushered the children inside.

When John came home later, she told him of the day's events and he said,

"I thought there were even more birds this morning. It's getting very weird."

"Ssssh," urged Elizabeth.

He ssshed and they heard the sound of children squealing and playing. John took up his heavy walking stick and went outside. It was dark and the lack of moon and proliferation of clouds made it seem darker. The noises were deafening and there was squealing and scurrying and snuffling.

"Foxes?" asked Elizabeth hopefully.

"No. Badgers I think."

The noises stopped and they went inside, more chilled than usual.

"I don't like Staley Bridge," said Elizabeth.

"You don't like anywhere," noted John and he slammed the door.

On Saturday night while Elizabeth prepared the children for their baptism by bathing them and making their best clothes presentable, an unearthly noise from outside stopped her.

John was with his pals at the inn but had promised to come home early. John was not a heavy drinker and would often only take a few drinks before returning. Perhaps it was because she was alone and peaceful that the noise shook her so much, but she was also freezing cold and shaking.

She looked out of the window and saw the tree aglow. She realised that the moon had come from behind a cloud and although only a fresh moon, it still had enough light to silhouette the hundreds and hundreds of birds sitting in the branches. Charity began to cry and so Elizabeth picked her up and went outside as if in a trance. Edwin was fast asleep and she felt safe doing so.

"Come on baby girl," she said. "Let's go and see what the moon is doing."

The moon was doing nothing, but the badger come fox come creepy noise making mammal was scuffing about in the hedgerows and squealing and clicking as it did so. Elizabeth drew Charity tighter and Charity panted in fear.

"Mama, please get Papa. I don't like the noises."

The starlings began to chirrup and then louder and louder their noises. They soon drowned out the scuffing noises and the women put their hands to their ears.

"I hate you. I hate you!" shouted Elizabeth to the starlings.

John appeared in the lane and made her jump even more.

"Stop saying you hate things Lizzy. Thoughts make things happen and bad thoughts…"

"… make bad things happen."

Lord, her husband could be annoying when he wanted to be. But she calmed down a little and the noises reduced so she calmed down some more and the chirruping stopped.

"See," he said gently and pushed her back in the house.

They were up, dressed and shutting their front door on their way to church by 8 o'clock the following morning. The starlings had begun chirruping at first light and when the family began walking past the tree, they tweeted as they had never done to date. How so many starlings could stay on the tree and it not collapse was unanswerable. The anxiety levels of the Prideaux family were very high and their neighbours stared at them as they walked into the church.

Baptising was done and hymns sung and yet the starlings could be heard above them all. None of the congregation kept attention on any part of the service and were glad to leave at the end. Everyone filed out and one by one they looked at the oak tree. The starlings were hopping up and down and leaves were falling.

As John and his family walked out of the church, the flock rose as one and soared into the sky. It was an awesome sight as they swooped and swirled as one.

Elizabeth and Charity became separated from John and Edwin as they became hypnotised.

This was a mistake. The flock came as a black cloud along the street and soon covered Charity and her mother. The other villagers screamed and ran to what they felt was a safe distance. John ran towards his wife and then saw that the baby was vulnerable and put him in the arms of a retreating woman he knew. He could no longer see his wife and daughter, just a fog of sparkling black wings and sharp little beaks which shredded his skin as he tried to grab his family. The birds swirled upwards and as they tornadoed towards the sky he saw that his family had gone with them.

"Demons!" shouted the parson as he fell to his knees in the lane.

"She must be a witch!" shouted the Edwin holding woman and she handed the child back to John as though he were on fire.

John cried and held the baby close. He looked into the sky and the birds and his wife and daughter had vanished. The villagers walked away muttering and John went home automatically. There were no starlings in the tree and no badger noises in the hedgerows.

He opened the front door and went in, unsure of his next step. Edwin was asleep in his arms and so he decided to lay him in his crib and find him some milk to warm. He would wake and scream the place down when he was hungry and John didn't think he could stand that. He went into the kitchen and took out the milk pail, putting some into a pan and placing it on the stove, as Elizabeth always did.

Elizabeth - what has just happened?

He stirred the milk and the back door opened. A young neighbour Mary came in.

"Are you aright John?" she asked him.

"No. Here stir this for me and feed Edwin when he wakes will you? I have to go out and look for my family. I don't know what else to do."

"Yes of course. People are out looking for them now John. They haven't found anything yet. They are talking witches and demons already."

John slammed the spoon onto the table.

"This village is living in the past with its ridiculous beliefs."

"Don't be mean John. They are worried about your family and are giving up their Sunday to help you."

John felt ashamed of his outburst.

"I am sorry Mary. I feel as though I am in a dream."

A noise of something falling stopped their conversation and they ran into the other room thinking that Edwin had fallen. He was safely sleeping and so John, closely followed by Mary went into his own bedroom.

There laying side by side on the bed were Elizabeth and Charity. They were both quite dead and completely covered in speckled black feathers.

John fell into a dead faint.

Within two months he was married to Mary. After the wedding they decided to leave the village where tongues were wagging about the speed of the union. For John it was practical. He could not look after himself or a boy on his own, so he must marry and Mary was willing. The locals were talking witches still and Mary not being a native of the place but an import from Wakefield was deemed to be the one responsible for the terrible deaths of Elizabeth and Charity.

They moved to Nottingham where John had the promise of some work and their son Matthew was born nine months after the wedding. The work did not last long and soon they moved to Leeds where John had heard there that he could work on the new railway. They rented a back to back which was infested with rats and lice. They were thoroughly miserable and Mary and John bickered constantly. They had only been there a few weeks before John began noticing the starlings in one of the few trees he passed on the way to work. "Christ," he muttered to himself.

John was depressed but would never speak of it. He really did not understand what it was he felt. He knew he was tired and that he missed his family back in Chudleigh. He thought of them often and had once started a letter but he screwed it up and threw it into the fire. So much time had passed now and he didn't know what to say to them. How could he write, I want to come home, find me a job and a house. But that was never going to happen. He couldn't go back as a failure. That was what he felt about himself. He was a failure. He couldn't go back, so what was the point in writing?

The starlings were collecting and increasing daily, seemingly in line with his thoughts. They were silent, but he didn't want to wait for them to begin their chirrups.

When these feelings became too much for him, he decided the family should move town. He had always done that, ever since he got fed up with life in Chudleigh.

He couldn't escape the thought that Leeds was a horrible place. The house they rented in Saville Street was cramped, smelly and damp. But it was all they could get. Oh to be back home near the fields and the flowers and the hills. These closed in streets of Leeds with so many people was hard to take. It was so like London and Mary working hard looking after the babies in the stuffy dark room was too hard to watch and he went to the inn at the end of the street.

There was less work on the railway than he had been given to believe and so John told his family that they would be moving to London. He was sure that his brother Peter would find them a place and some work. There would be more prospects for them down in London, he said.

That was an untruth. It was the starling tree warning him of trouble ahead and he didn't want to face it.

There had been too many bad thoughts, John could see that now.

Thoughts are things.

John did not feel close to his boys. He couldn't understand them and Mary did not help with her nagging tongue. He was aware that he had turned her into this nagging woman as he became more closed down. He hardly communicated with her and she was left with little alternative but to nag. And every day more birds came to the tree.

The day they left Leeds in 1849 and moved to 52 Boston Place in Christchurch, St Marylebone in London the birds screamed and squealed in the tree in the small field at the end of the street. They left early one morning without telling the landlord or their friends and John told his family to get to the railway station   before the birds woke. Mary did not argue, having felt the same feelings of unease. As the train pulled out of the station and the dawn broke, they watched a dark cloud begin to follow the train. They noticed some of their fellow early travellers looking out of the windows and pointing.

The cloud moved as fast as the train and some of the starlings began to land on the roof with a thud. Passengers just started a little with the first few bangs, but soon became more uneasy as the noises continued. Thud, thud, thud was quickly followed by scratching and chirruping and after only a minute or two the windows were covered in flapping birds and it was impossible to see out.

People were screaming and shouting for the guard and banging on the windows to scare away the birds. The guard arrived and tried in vain to take charge of a situation he had no experience of and no training for. The carriage was rocking and the well-travelled guard became red faced and panicky with this new experience.

John asked, "Will the train go faster? We might shake the birds off."

"As soon as we leave Leeds we will speed up. I have never seen this before. Have you?"

"I have seen starlings do odd things before but never on a train that is true."

The birds were making serious marks on the window glass and cracks were beginning to appear. Suddenly a bird came through the window and landed on the floor of the carriage, bloodied and screaming. Mary screamed and the boys cried. Passengers and guard alike held up hands in vain attempt to stem the flow of bloody starlings hurling themselves into the train.   It was still difficult to see the scenery outside as the corpses piled up inside.

Thousands and thousands came and as the train sped up it seemed some of the later starlings could not reach the train and gradually the pile of birds stopped. The windows now were free of birds but the broken glass iced with blood and ripped feathers were a reminder to what had just occurred.

The passengers helped the guard shovel the bloodied birds out of the way. Their journey was shortened by the chore and what else could they do?

When they landed at London, John took his family and ran out of the station. Some of the other passengers stayed a little longer in order to report about the strange phenomena they had experienced.

Their new house was a tenement and they shared the block with a stableman, a Coldstream Guard, an artificial flower maker and men who worked on the river. It was another noisy busy place. There were so many more people living there than in Leeds and if John was honest, more people than the last time he lived there. Even he felt under pressure now.

One day in 1850 he saw a huge fire in Lambeth and he thought again of home, of Chudleigh. The smoke and fire was visible for hours even though it was the other side of the river. He was surprised how much it had scared him and also how much he wanted to go home to Devon.

There was such poverty and cruelty and in order to survive a man needed to conform.

John again found himself doing work for unethical landlords and there was no way he could get to show his considerable talents as a carpenter.

One day he was walking along a side street, avoiding the scurrying people pushing their way past each other. Even though the sun was high in the sky, these streets seemed dark and menacing. Thick smoke and buildings built too close together and the constant need to have his head down in order not to trip up over others made every journey too stressful. Suddenly he was aware of a hand grabbing his arm. He looked up and saw the owner of the arm was a dirty looking man, smoking a pipe and standing in the alleyway.

"Hello Johnnie. Long time no see," he said.

"Sparks!" answered John. He recognized the man from his earlier years in London. He had been avoiding some of his former associates since his return as he did not want to go down that road again.

"You haven't been to see us. We missed you! Come with me now, we have a job for you."

"I already have a job; I don't need any more work!" John knew that he was in trouble now. Sparks looked more menacing than he had ever done all those years before. He followed him because he knew there was nothing else he could do.

Sparks led him down by the river through ever smaller streets. Soon they turned into an alleyway, climbed some rickety stairs which clung to the side of a brick building and scrambled through a door at the top which led into a dark room. A couple of nasty looking men stood guard outside this door, but moved aside when Sparks nodded to them.

"I got him," Sparks announced to the men inside.

"Hello Johnnie!" A buxom young woman moved towards John.

"Remember me?" Of course he did, this woman was well known to him. They had a dalliance when he first moved to London. Indeed Sally was the one who had introduced him to this gang of thieves in the first place.

"Hello Sally." She stroked his hair and he looked uncomfortably over her shoulder to see the others staring at him with either indifference or contempt. The room was very dark and the lamps lit on the table or the wall only seemed to accentuate their look of evil. This was not a good place to be. There was a nasty smell of urine mixed with sweat. Then John noticed a squeaking noise.

There was a young boy at the back of the room and he appeared to have his hands tied up.

"Papa."

It was Matthew.

"What in the hell are you doing with him?" John turned on his former associate.

"We just want you to know that we can do anything we want at any time we want. You joined us and you tried to leave. I told you then that it was not possible. You do as I say or Matthew will suffer. You know I mean it Johnnie boy."

John looked helplessly around the room and knew he was finished.

"Let him go. I'm back in." he said, now defeated.

"Off you go boy. Don't tell your mother about this." Sally had undone Matthew's bonds and was smoothing his hair back from his face.

"Go home Matt and stay there until I get home." Matthew ran out of the door determined that these people would not see him crying.

"Now then Johnnie boy, this next job involves your not inconsiderable skills. We both know what they are."
Sally had moved right next to John and was smiling at him.
John felt sick.
When John came home that night, Mary could not get any sense out of him. Matthew had come home several hours previously in a state of shock.
"What's happened to you both? John, the boy is only thirteen!"
"You soften that lad too much. Leave me alone woman!" He went upstairs, crashed about for a while and then came down and out of the front door.
It was several days before Mary got the truth out of her husband. She was horrified and particularly when she discovered that he had been doing illegal work already.
"Oh John, we must leave this place!"
But John would not.
Mary took Matthew the next day and they left London forever.
John moved to the Marquis of Granby cottages in St Pauls with his friend George Oliver and his family. Edwin married his Jane and moved away.
John never heard from Mary and as he had no idea where they were, that was the end of that. He told people that she was dead.
Whenever he saw a starling or indeed any type of bird sitting in a tree he would feel his heart race and he was

generally overcome with anxiety if any of them twittered or flew away.

This phobia rose again spectacularly during the spring of 1863 as John leant against a balcony which George had arranged for him to fix. He noticed starlings settling on the hedgerows opposite. They landed one by one until hundreds of them were there. They twittered and sang in a dreadful chorus and gradually began to synchronise their sound. As they did so, the tune became one continuous hum which caused the people John saw on the streets to put their hands over their ears and scurry away.

He felt his heart race and he couldn't concentrate. He pushed against the balcony in panic and the rail gave way with an almighty crack. John fell to the ground and lay still. He knew that he could not move and guessed that he had broken his back.

Some men came running towards him shouting, "Mate, are you alright?"

John thought of Chudleigh and his parents and the day of the fire and as he did he was back there. He was running through the streets from school to find his home. There was his mother standing on the step of the cottage. He hugged his mother as if he would never let her go and she hugged him back. He went into the cottage and saw his siblings sitting around the table eating as his father came into the room.

"Come on in son," his father said.

"Why the starlings?" John asked his hallucination.

"Baby stars my little boy. I told you that good thoughts and deeds went to make stars and bad thoughts and deeds went to make baby stars that turned into black birds unless they were looked after. Don't you remember? Only a joke John, only a joke..."
The men stood around the broken body of the carpenter.
"Stupid old fool, leaning on broken wood like that," said one and they heaved him onto a cart to take his body to the undertaker.

CHRISTMAS AT THE WORKHOUSE

featuring Matthew Prideaux 1838 -1888

"Why do you want to talk to me?" asked Matthew of the young woman sitting by his head and holding pen and paper.

Miss Ellen Young, school mistress at the Hunslet Union Workhouse, put down her pen and considered her answer.

"Because Mr Prideaux, I am writing a journal of the happenings at this place. I write down my observations and thoughts and opinions but I so rarely have an opportunity to take notes from someone who is experiencing the troubles here."

"I would imagine that you speak to all of the inmates?" he answered breathlessly, for Matthew was suffering from Phthisis.

"I do sir but most are either too sick, angry or unable to process and reveal their true thoughts."

"Why do you think that I might be none of those things?"

"I overheard the way you spoke to Mrs Wilson." Miss Young lowered her eyes in case they betrayed the utter contempt she felt towards the incumbent Workhouse Matron. "You spoke as an educated man might."

"I am barely educated Miss, although I have always read as many books as I can lay m hands on."

"Your parents were well educated?" she asked tentatively. Some of the unfortunates who found themselves relying on the poor county handouts were not always the God- allocated underlings which some of the charitable people cared to imagine they were.

Ellen Young had become a non-believer during her time at the Workhouse, although her initial desire to work there had come from similar charitable beliefs. She wanted to help the poor unfortunates whom she had seen evicted from cottages they could no longer pay for due to loss of a job or the death of the family head. Now homeless and often sick and aged, they must take themselves and their few possessions into the workhouse. There, their possessions were taken from them in order to contribute to their care and families were split up at the door, often never to communicate in this life again. Ellen found it traumatic when aged couples were ripped apart while half hugging in a final goodbye. Children were taken screaming from their crying mothers, the older ones later sitting straight backed and starving in her classroom, eager to make a good impression on the soft and perfumed teacher.

If God existed everywhere Ellen thought - He did not exist in a workhouse. Therefore He did not exist.

"My father was educated, not my mother, but she was a kind and resourceful woman as was my late wife. Both are long dead and my children are unable to look after me now."

"I see that from your records Mr Prideaux, although I believe your family have tried."

"They have, particularly my eldest daughter and the other children have been split up among my family. I will be dead soon and they will not have to worry about me."

This was said with little emotion and Ellen felt for him.

"Will you talk to me for a while?" she asked.

"Won't you get into trouble Miss? The bosses will not want you here and the nurses will come and make you leave."

"Not tonight Mr Prideaux, for it is Christmas night and they are all stuffing their faces with the food and drink that should be given to the residents here. I was invited but said I had a headache and have instead decided to walk about the place and talk to the people."

"Are you not afraid Miss?"

"Of the residents? No not at all. They will not harm me and to be honest most are locked up for the night."

"Except for us in the hospital?"

"Yes. You are all deemed too ill to go and observe their dreadful gluttony."

"In the style of Oliver Twist?"

"I knew I was right Mr Prideaux. I knew you were an educated man."

"Education matters not when you are about to die," he answered ruefully.

"Do you think so? I do not agree. I have a friend who has been to India and there they believe that the soul moves on to another life and takes all that has been learnt with it. And so we continue until we reach enlightenment."

"I have read about it. It is about keeping your mind aware as you die. Or something like that," said Matthew.

"Something like that," said Ellen.

She adjusted her chair in order to move it nearer to Matthew's head and then passed him a drink of water.

"What is your earliest memory Mr Prideaux?"

"If we are to talk, call me Matthew."

"I will Matthew and you must call me Ellen, unless anyone else is listening."

They laughed. The silence in the ward was only broken by coughing or moaning and neither call was being attended by the absent staff.

"My earliest memory was being carried through the streets of Leeds clutching my mother and my elder brother walking alongside. I know that my mother was very cross. She held me under one arm and the feeling was of great discomfort. I think she was going to fetch my father from the inn and somehow shame him for allowing us to go without while he drank. My father John worked as a joiner. His family had been master carpenters for several generations and his grandfather was sought out by wealthy homeowners to do exquisite work on the timbers around their homes. But my father struggled to find any work at all. He did some work on the houses of his neighbours in the pay of the landlord. But the landlords did not want to pay much money and expected John to merely 'make do'. The neighbours however took it upon themselves to blame John for the amount of work he did. They blamed his shoddy workmanship and laziness instead of blaming their landlord for his meanness. John found it very difficult and often sought solace in drink, spending the little money the family had available."

An unfamiliar noise in the doorway of the ward caused them both to turn round, fearing Matron. However there was nothing to be seen which could be illuminated by the lamps. Ellen turned back to her questioning,

"Have you got any really terrible memories?"

"I do remember a dreadful train journey from Leeds to London when the train was attacked by thousands of birds and left me and the rest of the family terrified of the awful flapping things for life. But then arriving in London I found out that was an even more terrifying place to be."

"When was this?" she asked.

"1850 Miss, very Dickensian and cruel. The streets were covered with horse manure and mud and there were people and horse drawn hackney cabs everywhere. Raw sewage ran into the same water which we also used for drinking. Prostitutes, beggars and thieves abounded on every street and commonplace crime and murder made it no place for a sentimental person. Cattle and sheep were driven through the streets and then sold and slaughtered in the markets. The slaughter men and butchers walked about the town, still covered in blood and successfully scaring the little children. There was a constant deafening noise and smog and smoke hung constantly over the city. Most people stank and the streets became just as smelly with each rain shower."

"How did your mother cope?"

"She hated it. I managed to find some work alongside Father and Edwin as a joiner's mate. We worked in many of the hovels where the poor lived and worked. All the repairs were paid for by landlords who were hard taskmasters. Father no longer seemed to care. Edwin was very like our father and the two of them often teased and upset the more sensitive me." Matthew smiled at the sad memory.

Ellen continued her jottings and smiled encouragement at the patient.

"I was only seventeen and Mother and I decided to leave London and seek our fortunes elsewhere. Mother took the money she had been saving for the last few years from its hiding place behind a brick near the fire place. She wrapped it safely in a small bag and hid it under her skirts. We stole away one Sunday morning and lost ourselves amongst the early market traders and late night revellers still on their way home. I vaguely remember my father standing in the doorway but saying nothing. The destination was Leeds where Mother had relatives and after two weeks of walking and hitching rides we arrived here. Mother knocked on the door of an old friend and through her contact we soon moved into the small house on Atkinson Street. I found work as a carpenter and Mother as a seamstress. This arrangement worked well for almost three years."

"Was that when your mother passed?" asked Ellen kindly.

"No Miss. It was then that I met my future wife Sarah Jackson when I was doing some joinery in the factory where she worked. Sarah decided that I was the one for her and she set out to catch me. Sarah's family had moved from Lincolnshire, where her father worked on the land. Work was hard to find there and he moved the family to Leeds where he knew there would be work. He worked with blue slate, his boys in the brickyard and his girls at the mill. When we married we all lived at Atkinson Street with mother. When Mary became ill with bronchitis, Sarah nursed her as she would her own mother."

"That was when she died?"

"She died on 4th May 1864 with Sarah at her side. Then a few months later Mary Emma was born fit and well. It was then that the hauntings began."

"Sorry. What?" Ellen held her pen mid-air, unsure of what she had just heard.

"Mother began to appear at the side of the new baby. We thought that she was just looking after her."

"You saw your mother's spirit?"

"You don't believe that to be possible Miss? And yet you are living in a workhouse all these years where the corridors are roamed daily by the tormented spirits of passed inmates?"

Ellen did not know how to answer without making herself look foolish.

"Well, I don't know. I'm not sure. I have heard stories naturally and some of the children pretend that they see ghosts walking about in the dark trying to scare them."

"It's not protected though, is it? I've seen them here regularly." Matthew slumped back against the pillows as though ready to sleep."

"Do you want me to leave, Mr Prideaux? Is this too much for you?"

"No, Miss. I might as well tell you my story as no one else is interested. Now that I have the time to tell my children our family story, they aren't able to come here and listen. Or they probably don't want to."

The noise by the doorway sounded again. It was a shuffling and knocking combination which was enough to cause Ellen to stand up and walk towards it.

"Hello?" she asked.

A small woman, dressed in workhouse garb came out from behind the curtain. She was bent over at right angles and leaning heavily on a thick wooden stick.

"Should you not be asleep now?" said Ellen.

The old woman stared at Ellen from underneath her greasy fringe. She spat and vanished into the dark.

Ellen walked back to Matthew's bed.

"You saw her didn't you?" he asked.

"Of course."

"Well, she's a ghost," Matthew said and smiled broadly. Ellen noticed that his smile lit up his grey and thin face. He must have been very handsome before he got sick, she thought.

Ellen sat back down.

"How many children do you have?"

"We had a few," answered Matthew. "After Mary Emma, Sarah had two miscarriages and then carried a son successfully to term. We named him Edwin John after my brother who I miss even now. Another daughter was born and then George after two more miscarriages. Then, during the next ten years Sarah had several miscarriages and five further children, including twins."

Ellen acknowledged the way Matthew spoke. His speech neither matched his situation nor his last address, but Ellen declined to mention the fact. Matthew Prideaux must descend from different stock than she had first imagined.

"Did they all live Matthew?"

"No sadly. Charles was born sickly and was not expected to live. His twin Eliza died after reaching almost two years old and having constant nursing from her mother. Sarah had another miscarriage just before Eliza died. Sarah dealt with the doctors and the funerals. The children are buried in paupers' graves and flowers picked from the grass verges as none could be afforded. Sarah grieved for each and every one of our lost children. I would not talk about them, although I grieved in my own way."

"That is terrible Matthew. How I wish there was a more accessible route to doctors and nurses for the poor."

"It's a pity that the doctors we have don't know what they are doing most of the time. They are so arrogant and sure of themselves and blame God when their patients die so easily. They fail day in and day out and expect to be treated with deference and respect."

Ellen nodded; she had as much respect for doctors as she did for the clergy. She pulled her shawl over her shoulders as there was a sudden cold draught.

"Are you warm enough Matthew?"

"I am fine. I expect you are feeling the spirit presence."

"Very funny. You can't frighten me."

"I am not trying to Miss. As I told you, there were plenty of ghosts in my house, but there are even more here at the workhouse. It seems to me that no one who died has left the place."

"They probably don't realise that they are dead."

"That's what I think. They haven't noticed that they have left the prison."

"Why did your passed family stay you with after they died?"

"Because they didn't want to leave or didn't know they were dead. We never did any of the silly tricks that others did to prevent the spirits of the deceased following them home from the graveyards."

Ellen nodded and made some notes. She was well aware of the customs but knew that these practices did not occur at the workhouse. The bodies were buried in the workhouse plot outside the grounds. First they were placed in a cheap coffin where they were squashed in tightly. Then the coffins were kept in a side building until there were enough to fill the hole which was then filled in and left unmarked. It was no wonder that a spirit did not want to go there.

As if reading her thoughts Matthew said,

"The bodies are often kept so long here prior to burial that the spirits leave the body and begin to roam the corridors again. At home there was one time when one of our babies had to stay in his little coffin for two weeks until there were enough to join him in his hole in the ground. "

Ellen shivered again.

"Do you really think that is what happens Matthew? That there are ghosts walking the corridors?"

"Of course. Surely you know that Miss Young, you have been here long enough?"

Yes she did know. She could feel them now, surrounding her and listening to their talk. They must feel particularly free to roam tonight with the rats away at their Christmas celebrations.

"That means the same thing is happening at all the workhouses around the country. They all do the same thing with those who have passed."

"And schools and universities and hospitals. There will be spirits all over them and I doubt they will ever leave because they won't understand."

"That is a frightening thought," said Ellen.

"I don't know so much. It depends where you imagine that leaving here at death takes you to. I think it takes you to where you expect to go."

"Where do you think you are going Matthew?"

"Because I am dying now?" he chuckled.

"I don't wish to offend you Matthew, but yes I suppose. A death sentence does rather focus the mind."

"I want to go back to Devon or Cornwall when I leave. And I do not believe for one minute that I need to go up to Heaven or down to Hell dependent on how good some ridiculous priest thinks I have been. I hope I find my Sarah and my mother there, but if I don't I shall begin again in my root country. Where will you go Miss?"

Ellen didn't need to think. "I am leaving here after Christmas although they don't know yet. I shall go to India with my friend and meet the great spiritual teachers there. Perhaps I shall stay there after I die this time round."

"Good for you Miss."

There came the sound of several heavy feet marching down the outside corridor towards the ward door. Ellen started,

"Oh. Why are they coming back tonight? I thought they would be feasting until well after midnight."

She began to rise from her chair.

"No wait here, you won't be seeing a warm body coming through those doors."

The ward doors swung open as if pushed by a firm hand. The footsteps continued but were made by no visible person. They marched along the centre of the ward and went out through the end doors which swung open in a similar way.

"They are active tonight. Why?" asked Ellen.

"It's Christmas so the veil is thinner and there are no bosses about."

"Oh, I see. I think I see. It's quite exciting isn't it?"

"Do you want me to come and haunt you when I go Miss?"

"Not really. Or perhaps, I don't know. Just don't make me jump!"

Matthew laughed and beckoned to her to continue her questioning.

"Before I fall asleep and join the marching feet," he said.

"What happened to your children?"

"Agnes was sent away to live with my maternal aunt Mary and her husband George Kitchen at the Oatlands Inn. You know she went on the stage along with two of her Kitchen cousins?"

"Oh where?"

"Lots of plays at the Theatre Royal in Leeds and they had some dog act called 'Messrs Lamb and Kitchen and their Wonderful Dogs.'," he said with a flourish.

"I saw them!" said Ellen with genuine interest. "They were really very clever."

"They were indeed, Agnes always loved dogs. She still has them and she loves the stage. I expect she will be haunting the Theatre Royal when she goes."

"And what about the others?"

"When little Eliza died, I really noticed a difference in Sarah. She became pale and tired and had large black rings under her eyes. We were used to her singing and laughing and never being depressed. That had all changed now. We moved to 22 Ambler Yard in Holbeck as Sarah had decided that the last house was bad luck. I told her she was being stupid, but in truth I was more superstitious than my wife. It was me who put some lucky charms in the chimney breast and bedroom in order to ward off evil. I probably saw our ghost children more than Sarah did but I would never admit that. Then we only lived there for less than a month because Sarah's cough became worse. I have an idea that the dead children and my mother had been keeping us safe."

"What was the matter with Sarah?"

"She coughed up blood, the usual problem. She told me she knew that she was dying when we sat in our tiny kitchen one evening. She wouldn't go the doctor, because they never help. It was the end of summer 1884. The August evenings were still warm and the muggy air made Sarah's cough worse. By the beginning of September Sarah had taken to her bed. She was being nursed in turn by our girls but she was fading fast. 'Look after the babies Mary 'she told our eldest daughter. 'Of course I will Mama,' she answered. 'But you will get better.' 'I won't Mary, I am worn out. My spirit is already halfway gone. I saw my dead babies in the room last night.' Mary did not know what to say. Sarah told Mary that when she was dreaming that she saw many little children come into her bedroom after I went to sleep and they held out their fat little hands to her."

"Was she scared?" asked Ellen.

"Mary said not and I don't think Sarah was. She had a great faith unlike me. She said to Mary, 'Don't worry about me, my darling girl. All will be well.' And then she closed her eyes and died. There was a huge smile on her face and she looked like a girl again. It was 21st September 1884."

Matthew looked up from his bed to the pretty young woman jotting down his ramblings. Ellen noticed and asked him if he needed food or water.

"Water please but if you have any spare food then give it to the children."

"I will – I do. What happened to the children when you came in here?"

"Mary Emma wanted to marry her friend Arthur soon after Sarah died, but stayed looking after me instead, I got sick and could not work and so they all clubbed together to look after me. I signed myself in here so that they could have a life. She will marry him as soon as I die, I should imagine .George managed to find lodgings in Grape Street and Edwin lodged with his girlfriend and her mother. William and Thomas live with Mary and will live with her after she marries. They don't need me."

"I am sure they do need you."

"Perhaps, but if I hurry up and leave here, they will soon forget about me. I say, why don't we have a bit of an adventure before the nasty people get back?"

Ellen closed her journal and said,

"Adventure? What did you have in mind?"

"Let us get the spirits moving and marching to their Christmas meal."

"Wonderful idea, but how?"

"Fetch that wheelchair over here and while you do that, I shall pee in a bottle."

Ellen jumped up and left him to his business and brought the chair back once he said he was ready. She wrapped his legs in his blanket and put a pillow behind his back.

"Right, now take me to the morgue."

"No! Why? I am too frightened!"

"Well I am not frightened for I shall be there soon enough, so push me please."

"I don't think that is a good idea."

"I didn't argue with you when you wanted to write my story in your journal, did I?"

Ellen thought for only a moment and began to push hm. For if she was intending to leave the employ of the Workhouse and go to India with John in search of enlightenment, then she really should be prepared to take some risks at home.

She wheeled Matthew up and down corridors, conscious that they were being watched by live eyes and dead. The live ones peeked and sneaked as they went past but were much too fearful to follow. Past experience had taught them that to interfere in anything outside of their remit was – well, it wasn't worth it.

The dead ones seemed to scoot behind them and then every so often they would see a shadow or shape hiding in a stairwell or doorway,

"Ignore them," said Matthew.

"I am trying to," Ellen answered.

"I am so near the veil now Ellen that I can see and experience much more than you can. Most dying people are but they spend all of their time worrying about how ill they feel and whether Jesus or their mother will be there to meet them. They should embrace the process and take control of it."

"How?"

"By noticing their perceptual changes. This isn't the only life any of us have lived or will live. If we don't pay attention to our intentions and feelings when we are dying, we will go to where those scary feelings match."

"You are saying we can control where we go?"

"Of course we can. I never want to enter a prison or a workhouse or anywhere restrictive again and now I know that I am able to do it."

They arrived at the morgue and Ellen turned the wheelchair round and pushed the doors open with her bustle.

They were inside.

To her horror she saw that there were four bodies lying on top of each other on a large table in the corner of the room.

"No respect you see," muttered Matthew.

"I do see. I think it is disgraceful. What now? Do we perform some kind of spell?"

"Not at all, spells only strengthen our thoughts. Once you decide what you want to do just expect it to happen. It will."

"I see. So what shall we do now?"

"This."

Matthew poked one of the bodies and Ellen saw dust rise from the shroud which surrounded it. But of course it wasn't dust - it was a spirit. The dust clouded above the body and then morphed into four separate shapes.

"Ladies and gentlemen, I want you all to collect some of our other spirit friends and move on to the room where the Master and his family and staff are stuffing their big fat faces with food that would have done you some good in your last days of your life."

The spirits flew and spun around Ellen and Matthew and soon the marching sounds began again.

"They are coming!" said Matthew in a theatrical voice.

The mortuary door swung open and nothing but marching boots entered the room. The new ghosts swirled above them turning the room green and glowing. The marching feet must have about-turned because the noise was retreating back up the corridor. Matthew beckoned Ellen to follow them and she did.

As they neared the Master's quarters some minutes later, the marching was in complete unison and the floor and walls vibrated with the sound. Matthew grabbed Ellen's arm and told her to push him into the stairwell from where they could perceive the scene better.

Master Atkins opened the door and looked up and down the corridor.

"There is nothing here!" he shouted back into the room.

Then he was pushed aside and thrown to the ground as the crowd of marching boots thrust past him and the green glowing cloud followed just before the door was slammed shut by a better-late-than-never servant.

The screaming and wailing which came from the room caused Ellen to put her hand to her ears and Matthew to laugh.

"We should go," she said.

"Not yet."

The doors slammed open again and people began streaming out, grasping their coats and their bags. They were screaming and terrified as they ran towards the main doors. Master Atkins followed them out exclaiming to his servants that the food and drink must have been poisoned and that it must be removed immediately.

"Give it to the dammed inmates," he shouted. "Let them hallucinate!"

"Christmas dinner for the workers!" laughed Matthew.

Ellen quickly pushed him back to his ward and got him safety into bed.

She tucked him in and said, "It has been a pleasure to meet you Matthew. We shall not meet again for I leave in the morning."

"Live your life well Ellen. I shall visit you in India - in your dreams."

She turned down his lamp and walked to the door clutching her journal. There under the sign informing the visitor that this was the infirmary, she turned back for a final look. Matthew was surrounded by a warm orange glow reminiscent of a Christmas fire. There were men, women and children looking down on him, some tucking him in and some stroking his brow. A woman whom Ellen assumed was his beloved mother held his hand and smiled at him like the angel she was. Ellen knew he was safe forever now and she cried softly for this enlightening scene that she would never be able to describe adequately to another soul.

CHERRY RIPE

featuring George Prideaux 1871 – 1926

Cherry-Ripe by Robert Herrick

Cherry ripe, cherry ripe,
Ripe I cry,
Full and fair ones
Come and buy.

George Herbert was born 23rd August 1871 at 5 Gorse Street, Hunslet. He was the fourth child of Matthew and Sarah Prideaux and their second son. He was also my great grandfather and I have his papers in my possession. I have transcribed some of the entries here - the ones I feel bring this particular event to life.

Some of the writings I have put together without dates as George wrote later in reference to his childhood and I felt it would complicate the tale to date the journal entries rather than remain chronological.

His son Clifford took possession of an oak chest which was always in George's house and although locked and no key found, Clifford broke it open. Inside he found papers and diaries and letters which he briefly read through before returning them to the chest. He also found a cigarette case and snuff box, within which were some pits which he guessed were cherry. Clifford remembered his father's interest in cherry tree cultivation.

I will relate through this story how this interesting little hobby began.

Soon after George was born, the family moved to 5 Essex Street.   Next door was home to Elizabeth Ogden who lived there with her sister and her niece. Elizabeth was deaf and dumb and received unfortunate attention from the children in the street about her affliction.

"I don't want to ever hear that you have been cruel to Miss Ogden," said George's mother Sarah. Her own sister was deaf and she knew from experience how horrid people could be.

Ten year old George said, "Mam! We don't do things like that!"

But of course they did. They followed Elizabeth as she walked to her charring job shouting things which they knew she could not hear. Once, George had barged into the toilet which the two families shared. He had knocked, but of course she could not hear and she silently screamed in shame at being caught skirts up and sitting on the well-scrubbed wooden seat. George had been initially embarrassed and then found it extremely funny when he recounted the event to his friends.

He felt ashamed when he was told that the story had been relayed around the neighbourhood and Elizabeth would no longer speak to him.

George was present when three of his siblings Arthur, Charles and Eliza died. He was so excited when the twins were born and then to see Charles succumb so quickly and be followed to the grave by Eliza who died before her second birthday affected him deeply. Eliza was deformed and constantly sick and in pain. After her birth, George never picked on the neighbour again.

George worried constantly about the health of his mother. She often seemed tired and careworn. Her hair was prematurely grey and her face lined and pale. She coughed constantly and the coughing seemed worse during the night and in the morning. Even the smoke from the fire upset her.

When the third baby died, George really noticed a difference in his mother.

They moved to 22 Ambler Yard in Holbeck as Sarah had decided that the last house was bad luck. Matthew told her she was being stupid, but George knew that his father was more superstitious than his mother because he had seen him put something near the chimney. George saw the ghosts too but when he had tried to tell his mother his father had stopped him, citing her frailness. They were there for less than a month because Sarah's cough became worse.

Sarah did not recover from all this illness and death and died herself of capillary bronchitis from which she had suffered from for two weeks before she succumbed on the 21st September 1884. She was 46.

Matthew stayed at this address for a while before he too died at the Hunslet Union Workhouse on the 21st January 1888 of Phthisis

George's family was destroyed and they were all forced to move to new addresses.

Mary Emma had been courting Arthur Kay and as soon as she nursed her mother and then her father to their deaths, they married. Mary Emma and Arthur moved into 24 Grape Street and took the two youngest boys, Thomas and William in. She looked after them until they married and moved to Leeds.

"I don't want any of you becoming drunks just because we are living next door to the Queens Inn," she told them.

George moved as a lodger down the road at 77 Grape Street with Elizabeth Catton and Hannah Holgate. A couple of years later he moved to No 89 where he could live alone and soon had new neighbours who moved into No 93. They had a lovely daughter called Mary Ann Hobson and the two married in St Silas Church in Hunslet on 21st January 1893, five years to the day of his father's passing.

His sister Mary Emma and her husband attended as witnesses along with his two youngest brothers.

Soon after marriage they left Grape Street and moved to 7 Burniston Court where I pick up his story in 'A Christmas Story'.

But now I have got a little ahead of the story I want to relate and we must go back to Grape Street. The small amount of background story above may help you understand how George could be led so easily into a mystery and was very kind at heart.

There was a public house on Grape Street called the Queens Inn. It was frequented by all type of regulars, some of whom worked at Armley Gaol.

On one occasion George was working for the landlord as a glass collector and when he had a slack time, he hovered around the guards and listened to their tales of the Gaol. He was often shouted away in order to attend to his work and he answered the call because he needed the pennies.

He had a chance to learn more when one called him over,

"Boy! You been listening to us stories have you?"

"No sir! Well yes sir – a little. I want to be a policeman so I was just interested."

"Police is it? We aint police, we are prison guards. We deal with the wrong 'uns after they been banged up."

"I know," said George.

"Oh, he knows!" said one guard.

"'e should make a good copper then!" laughed the other.

George wiped down their table - one of his allocated tasks.

"Do you do the hangings?" he asked.

"Hangings? No boy we don't do the hangings, Crown men does the hangings and let me tell you they are not very good at it."

"That's right, so make sure you don't murder no one cos you will end up swinging for half an hour before you die. It's not always a quick job."

George wiped the table as though he were trying to remove the paint from it.

"I am always good sir and I would never harm anyone, let alone murder them."

The men laughed heartily, enjoying their fun.

"I am sure you are. Now fetch us more drink before we die of thirst and if you are quick about it, I will tell you a tale that will keep you awake at night."

"Thank you sir," said George and ran away to the bar.

"Here you are," he said three minutes later. He had fetched ale, collected glasses and scampered back to the guards, anxious to hear their terrible tale before he lost them forever.

He gazed at the men with his big dark eyes.

"Sit by me 'ere," the bigger guard said, patting the bench.

The landlord shouted over to George.

"Give him five minutes boss!" answered the guard. "I knew his father!"

The landlord mumbled something but did not want to upset a prison guard, he might need his help one day.

"Did you know my father?" asked George.

"No, but I'm sure he was a good 'un."

George blushed and said, "Can you tell me your hanging story?"

"Impatient lad, aren't you? It was ten years ago in '76 when they were hanging John Johnson and they went through all the usual procedures and tests and everything worked fine. This hangman Thomas Askern was bad at his job and getting known for it."

"This turned out to be his last job," said his mate.

"It did and right that was too. I'm all for hanging murderers but not for being so cruel."

"What happened?" asked George breathlessly.

"They took him up the steps and led him on to the trapdoor where they finished strapping him and put the hood over his head. He didn't say anything to the crowd and then Askern put the rope round his neck and pulled the lever. Jones fell right through the trapdoor and so did the broken rope behind him."

George had not moved since the story began, eager to remember every detail.

"Was he dead?"

"No he wasn't. We had to go through the black curtains under the gallows to find him all moaning and struggling in his bonds with his hood on and the broken noose round his neck."

"So did you let him go free?"

"No, the law wants its Judgement. The law thinks it's God. We got the fellow a chair that one of the dignitaries had been parked on and let Jones sit by the gallows while they all looked for a better rope."

"That's horrible!" said George.

"It is and that's a fact. I felt a bit sorry for Jones so I gave him some cherries that I had in my pocket. The missus had given them to me to take to her mother, but I felt this man's needs were greater. He was real grateful and chewed on them until they had finished fixing the new rope up. Then we walked him back up the scaffold and they put the noose on him again.

He said to me, "These pits'll be worth a bit one day!" and they dropped him again. It took him nearly 5 minutes to die, the poor bugger."

"What happened then?" asked George.

"I went and fetched the pits. The poor man had been spitting them out all the time he was throttling the second time. I suppose I thought they would be valuable."

The guard took a snuff box from his pocket and opened it.

"Are they?" said George, peering into the box.

"No and they brought me nothing but bad luck I think. I'm going to throw them away," he said snapping the lid shut.

"Can I have them please?" asked George.

The guards looked at him and the landlord shouted, "George, get over here now or go home and don't come back again!"

"You had better go boy or you will lose your job," the big guard said.

George clutched his towel and stared at the snuff box. The guard threw it in the air and George caught it.

"Go on. Bugger off," said the guard.

And bugger off George did, with snuff box pocketed and a grin on his face.

Reading through George's notes I see that he researched cherry trees and how to grow them for quite some time before he finally put one pit in soil that he had specially prepared. He only dare do one at a time in case it didn't work. Once he had exposed the pit to cold then it seemed that it must germinate. He had ten cherry pits in total.

George waited six months before he was sure that the pit had not germinated and then had to wait until he could try again. He was luckier the second time around and a year later had a tiny little tree in a pot in his house. He planted another to be certain and soon had a second little tree. He used seven pits over the years and got five trees.

He had hopes of sweet cherries and he wished that he was able to show his parents what he had achieved.

By the time he married he was only able to keep one tree and so gave the others to people with gardens, but did not tell of their history.

He probably didn't want them to know what happened with the trees at night. His own tree was in a bigger pot and he pruned it to keep it small and kept it by the window or moved it out into the fresh air whenever he could. The tree was healthy and responsive.

Now here is where the story becomes stranger. George writes in his journal that he would talk to the tree to encourage its growth and the tree would answer him back. George would ask questions with mainly yes or no answers and the tree would shake its branches in response.

At night when it was dark and silent George would hear whispers coming from the tree and as he tried to understand what was being said he realised that it was the twice-hanged man talking to him. It seemed that being hung once sends a person to their next life and being hanged twice keeps them in this life.

This night set off a series of changes in George's life.

He researched and asked questions about the twice-hanged man at Armley and became fearful that the murderer could now somehow control his thoughts. In order to protect himself George placed a crucifix in the soil next to the tree. He began to imagine that the tree was watching him – it certainly seemed to perk up and shake whenever he walked back into the house.

It was also getting quite big and friends and neighbours said he was silly to keep it in the room with him for everyone knew that plants take all your oxygen and can kill you when you are asleep. George wasn't dead yet and he had a great attachment to the tree and in spite of constant complaining from his wife Mary, he continued to look after it carefully.

The tree began to produce fruit and George collected the cherries and told his wife that the pits must never be swallowed nor thrown away but washed and dried and placed in the snuff box. Mary didn't complain at harvest time for the tree did produce a huge amount of cherries, far more than would seem likely for such a small tree. Of course the spring blossom was wonderful and during the early Spring through to fruiting season, neighbours congratulated George on his beautiful tree which brought colour and scent to the grim street. In the Wintertime George dragged the pot into the back kitchen and covered it with a sack to protect it from frost.

From time to time he would visit his other trees and noted that gradually they had failed and died off despite a far superior environment in which to grow.

George's tree continued to thrive and did not mind its life in a tiny and crowded Leeds house. In fact the tree loved it there. On more than one occasion someone had tried to steal or damage the tree either with or without witnesses. They soon regretted the attempt.

One woman had jealously decided that the fruit should be hers and under cover of darkness took a basket and crept up to the tree. She took hold of a pair of cherries and pulled them lightly ready to place them in her basket. Later she told a friend that that tree began to pull back and soon she was in a two-handed battle with a small cherry tree on a late Summer evening. She swore that she heard the tree growl and then say, 'Clear off you thieving bitch.' She let go and ran back home crying.

Two drunken friends of George's thought it would be a lark to pull the tree from its pot and throw it across the street.

"Summat up with a bloke who wants to play with flowers," one said and grabbed hard hold of the tree. He fell back to the ground screaming.

"What's up?" asked his mate.

"It just bit me!" he said.

"Sure it did!" and his mate grabbed the tree.

He felt the pain but unlike his mate was unable to let go. He shouted and swore and tried to escape. It took half a minute before the tree released its grip and he could stare at his cut and bleeding hands.

"It aint got thorns has it?"

"No! It's just smooth!"

"Well look at me hands!" The blood was flooding from his palms and they rushed home quickly to get help there. The man suffered infection and fever for the following week and then he died. His friend found it difficult to use his hands properly for the rest of his life.

Talk began after this episode and most would avoid the tree even when it was in full flower and sweet smelling, waving in the warm Spring breeze outside the front door of the Prideaux home.

A young man, keen to impress a pretty young girl and knowing nothing of the stories, crept to the tree with a small pocket knife eager to snip a few blossoms for a posy. He approached the tree in the dark and it snapped a branch at him so quickly that it knocked the knife from his hand and flicked it into his chest. Luckily the knife did not impale him too deeply and he ran away dripping blood.

Mary insisted that the tree be destroyed and thrown away but George was loathe so to do. Instead he rented a small garden orchard from a woman in Bramley village to whom he had given a cherry tree previously and the promise to plant more trees which would result in a crop of sweet cherries every year sealed the deal. She gave him permission to continue with his cultivation and there the tree went.

It appears that through the following many years, George spent a good deal of his time at the orchard treasuring his cherry trees and soon had ten producing fruit. As he brought each tree to harvest he kept many of the pits with which he could cultivate new trees. The trees were planted in his small orchard and the owner of Wellington House on Broad Lane enjoyed the results of his labour. Some of her friends wanted to buy young trees from him and he would allow that on odd occasions as the payment offered was more than he could afford to turn away. These sold trees neither fruited nor survived.

George often talked to his trees and he wrote that they talked back. He apparently told no-one about his chats.

He was convinced that the hanged man was reincarnated in the trees – all of the trees. George wrote about the life the man Jones had had and how his mistakes had led him to murder and his subsequent execution. Jones was grateful that George was planting and caring for the trees, because that meant he could still live. He wanted to protect George and his brother trees in order that he could stay alive. George wrote, 'Jones wants to live and I am the only person able to make that happen. He will never allow me to stop.'

It seemed he told Jones that he was thinking of spending less time at Bramley because it was becoming difficult to spare the hours. The trees would shake and the branches grab him and not let go as he walked past. George was becoming scared.

By 1900 George and Mary had five children, although little Ben died less than two years after his birth. He died of Diphtheria after suffering dreadfully for weeks. Convulsions finally took him to his maker on Christmas Eve 1899.

"Why does Jesus want all these little babies?" Mary cried. "He takes so many, why does he want my little Ben too?"

There could be no answer to this. The authorities insisted on a post mortem and he could not be buried until after 27th December when they decided he had in fact died of natural causes.

Mary Ann would never forget the boy's death. His little body stayed in the front room until it was walked down to Holbeck for burial. They had hardly any money, but Mary Ann insisted that some flowers were carried with his coffin. George brought Christmas roses from his garden orchard. Mary still felt Ben's presence around the house, but did not tell George as he would have laughed. George would not have laughed. He often saw his own dear mother when he felt particularly tense.

George told his trees about his upsets and he swore that he heard in a whispered tone,

"Stay here then George. You kill my beloveds and I will kill yours."

George promised to stay there when he visited Wellington House orchard on Christmas Eve 1902.

Their luck changed the following day when they welcomed baby Clifford into their family on Christmas Day.

"Jesus has sent you another son to take the place of Ben," said George to his wife. Another three children followed and Jane arrived nine months after Ben's death. Nine births and one death was a very good average for the time, but George wrote that it was because of the Jones cherry tree.

George continued to look after the trees for years and seemed to be getting more concerned about the control they had over his life. But he went to the orchard regularly and cared for the trees, always mindful of what he spoke about and told the Jones trees of interesting facts and news of the war and his children and their marriages and so forth.

By the summer of 1926 George was becoming ill and less able to go to the orchard. His friend at Wellington House was also ageing and she visited the orchard less and less. The hedges were becoming overgrown and the stone walls tumbling down a little more each month. It was beginning to resemble an unattended cemetery and Jones had no one left to remember him.

George knew that Jones was becoming angry, but told the trees that he was ill and tired and unable to function as he had to date.

"Die then," he heard the leaves whisper as he walked away.

One time on 13th October 1926 George Herbert went to visit his son and his new wife with Mary Ann. He had been very ill with bronchitis for several weeks. Mary Ann blamed his constant smoking and noted that George had coughed through the winters of most of their years together.

This particular morning had been different somehow. George looked very pale and coughed constantly.

"George do you think you should go today?"

"I said I would go and I will."

George sounded more forceful than he felt. He felt as weak as a kitten, but staying in bed had never made him feel better - not that he had ever had much time to laze about.

They set off and caught the tram to the railway station. Soon they were on board the train to Woodlesford which was not too far away and the journey took no longer than a few minutes. George was distant and seemed paler now than this morning.

After they walked to their son's house and spent a couple of hours there, his son and his wife were also very worried.

"I think you should see the doctor Dad. You seem so tired."

He knew his father had been laid off work for the last couple of days and that money was tight, but this was important.

"I will pay for the doctor, Dad."

George looked up and his eyes flashed.

"I am not so bad yet that I have to have a son of mine paying for me!" The anger made him cough all the more and everyone looked at him.

"Come on Annie, we are going home," he snapped.

His wife got up from her chair and gave her son a knowing look.

"Come and see us off George?"

"I'll come and see you to your own door, Mum. You should not travel on your own like this."

Mary was grateful and hugged her son. Annie waved them off from the doorstep and the three set off slowly to the station.

The bridge had to be crossed in order to get to the correct side of the tracks and the exertion seemed to set off George coughing.

"Have a cherry Dad, it's one of yours! The vitamins will do you good."

George took the fruit and accidentally swallowed the pit – something he had never done before. At the top step he staggered onto the bridge and leaned on the wall where he coughed for a minute or two before he went very pale and slumped to the floor, eyes closed.

"Dad!" shouted his son.

There was no answer and George watched helplessly as his father stopped breathing and died in front of them.

Mary Ann stood in shock, hands over her mouth and frozen to the spot.

George shouted over the edge of the bridge to the station porter to come and help. But it was no good. George Herbert Prideaux died that day.

The Prideaux family posted a notice in the Yorkshire Evening Post on October 15th.

PRIDEAUX Oct 15 at 100 Elland Road, Holbeck. George Herbert beloved husband of Mary Ann Prideaux, aged 55 years – internment at Holbeck Cemetery, Saturday at 3 leaving house 2.30. Friends please accept this the only intimation.

The funeral was arranged and over so quickly that Mary Ann and her sons had no time to cry. It was only as she stood over his grave, surrounded by her family and George's friends that it became real.

"We have had a talk, Mrs P and all his friends at the Club have had a whip round and are going to pay for a marble flower pot to go with the headstone. It is the least we can do."

Mary Ann stared at him and said nothing.

"Thank you very much," answered Clifford on her behalf. That is very good of you."

The funeral tea was held at the club and everyone went home. It was at this tea that Clifford took the journals and chest as mentioned at the beginning of this story.

The white marble headstone paid for by his family stands proudly in Holbeck Cemetery. When Mary Ann died in 1948, her remains were placed there also.

The white marble flower pot paid for by his many friends at the club stands alongside it.

However the engraving the friends arranged to put on there, states the name 'Priddo' – so much for his fame.

Clifford read through the journals a couple of times and put the stories down to his father's imaginative nature and his ability to tell a tall tale. Perhaps he had intended to send the writings to a publisher or just liked writing things down.

It was twenty five years later when Clifford and his wife and two daughters moved to a new house in Wood Lane in Bramley village when it dawned on him that the Wellington House which sat on the other side of the stone wall across the road from his front hedge housed the orchard his father had written about.

He vaguely knew the new owners and gained permission to look around the gardens citing Clifford's great interest in horticulture.

Clifford walked across the lawn from the front drive of Wellington House and broke through the brambles which covered a gate leading to an overgrown patch of ground. This was bordered by the stone wall, the wall which faced his house and Clifford swore he heard a voice saying, "About time too."

He walked on through the waist high grass, nettles and docks and noticed several cherry trees – all dead apart from one. The dead trees were bent over and broken and finished, but the central tree was still fruiting and healthy. This tree must be very old and Clifford wondered if this was where Jones now lived.

The tree responded to the touch Clifford gave as he stroked the cracked bark and he heard,

"Please save me Clifford, take the fruit and keep the pits. Plant them and keep me alive. I cannot go to Hell."

Clifford laughed at himself believing the voice and walked away.

"Please!" the voice begged.

Clifford turned back and opened the rucksack he had with him and filled it with cherries. The tree seemed to bow to him and said,

"Don't forget to plant them my friend."

Clifford watched as the leaves began to fall from the tree and spooked, he scurried back to the bramble covered gate.

He met some workmen striding towards him.

"Thanks for clearing the gate mate!" shouted one.

"Oh, going in there are you?"

"Sure are. The boss wants us to chop down the trees and bring him the wood. He needs it for his fireplace."

"There's still a live cherry tree in there," Clifford told them

"Won't be for long. He wants the whole orchard cleared so it can be opened up for grazing." The man held a rope in the air.

"It's to pull it down," he said. "Like a hanging!"

To the sound of screaming from the orchard, Clifford walked swiftly down the driveway and back up the road to his own house. Later that afternoon he watched from the wall as the workmen tied the rope around the top of the cherry tree and held it taut as they sawed at its trunk. Twice they pulled and the tree would not fall in spite of its injuries with the saw. The third time it came down with a terrible crack and Clifford watched as smoke shot out from the truck.

"Please!" he heard.

Clifford walked back to his house and went inside and asked Agnes to put the kettle on.

Clifford kept the dried cherry pits he had taken from the old tree and placed them into a wooden box which he kept separate to the other pits, still in their snuff box. He closed the chest and never planted the pits in his wonderful garden full of roses and London Pride.

I still have the pits...